Riley Rye, Private Eye

Written by
Kirsty Holmes

Illustrated by
Marianne Constable

Welcome to Cook Town.

Let's look around. This town really loves its food!

On Crumble Close, there lives a little girl and her big dog, Deputy.

But this isn't just any little girl...

This is Riley Rye, Private Eye.

Riley Rye, Private Eye - HQ

Have you got a problem that's making you blue?

Your cheese has been stolen and you can't make fondue?

Riley and Deputy will hunt out those clues!

Riley Rye, Private Eye, to the rescue!

(closed on Tuesday afternoons)

Riley and Deputy were in the HQ one morning, sharing a snack. It was a good morning. They were watching Chef Jeff's new TV show, The Perfect Pasty. Deputy sniffed the air. Was that the smell of... blueberries?

"BOO HOO HOO!" somebody cried from below. "Riley, are you there?"
It was Blueberry Sue. Blueberry Sue was a famous cook on TV. She was upset and also very blue. Her dress was blue, her hair was blue and even her lipstick was blue!
She cried into a huge blue handkerchief.
"Boo hoo hoo!" she sobbed. "I feel so blue!"

"Oh, Riley Rye!" Sue cried. "You have to help me! My pie recipe has been stolen! Oh, it's so unfair!"

"I thought you only cooked muffins?" asked Riley.

Blueberry Sue was the most famous muffin chef in Cook Town.

"I was about to begin my TV show, Blueberry Sue's Muffin Magic!, when I was hit with a brilliant idea! PIES!"

"Pies?" said Riley. Deputy looked up hopefully. He liked pies.

"Pies!" shouted Blueberry Sue. "They are the next big thing! Muffins are so last year."

"Just as I wrote my secret recipe down, the fire alarm went off!" Blueberry Sue wailed. "I didn't want to get fried, so I left my studio."
"A fire?" asked Riley.
"It was a false alarm," said Sue. "But when I got back, the recipe had gone! Oh, what am I going to do?"

"I'm sure that my pies will be the next big thing," Blueberry Sue sobbed into her handkerchief. "Someone must have stolen the recipe. Will you help me find out who?"
Riley looked at Deputy.
"Of course, Miss Sue. Quick, to the police station, Deputy!"

Riley went to find her dad, who was the police chief. This meant he was in charge of the police in Cook Town.

"Have we got a new case, Riley?" he said, putting on his smartest necktie.

"Yes! Quick, to the TV station!" Riley cried.

COOK TOWN
POLICE

At the TV station, Riley and Deputy started to look around. Dad wanted to meet the famous TV chefs, who buzzed about like busy bees. "Is that Cutie Pie? Wow! Can I say hi?" said Dad.

"Sure, Dad," Riley said. She tried to conceal a smile. "We've got this."

Blueberry Sue took them to her room.
"I was sitting here," Sue said, as she tried to remember. "I wrote the idea for the pie on a blue napkin."
Riley looked around. Everything in the room was blue.

"Wow. You really like the colour blue," said Riley.
"I even wrote the recipe in my blue lipstick," said Sue. "It's true – I do love blue!"
Hmm, thought Riley. That might be a clue...

Riley was looking at a strange yellow powder on the fire alarm when Dad came back. Could this be a clue?

"I've lined up the chefs for you, Riley," said Dad. "One of them might have some useful information."

"Thanks, Dad," said Riley. "You stay here with Blueberry Sue."

"Here. These muffins are to die for!" said Sue.

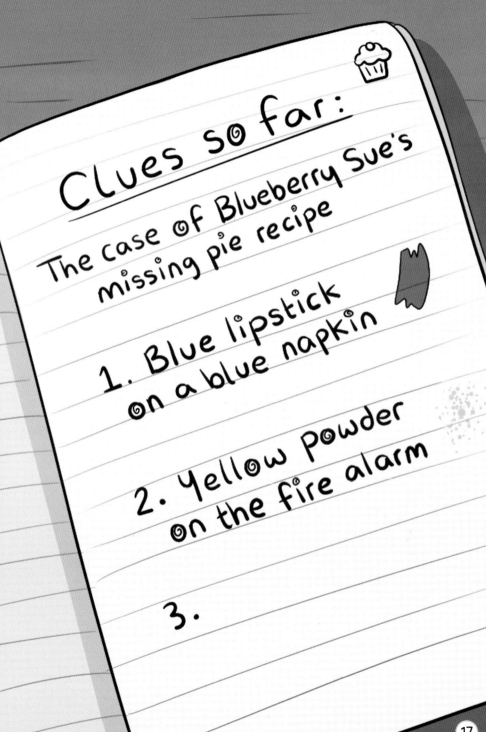

In the green room, Riley and Deputy found three famous TV chefs.

First was Chef Jeff, the pastry chef. He was shaking as he wept over a large lump of very wet pastry. The fire sprinklers had soaked everything.

Next, the lemon curd chef, Lemony Melanie.

Chef
Jeff

She was comforting Chef Jeff with a yellow tissue.

Blake Cupcake, the cake chef, was holding a tiny sugar flower in his giant hands, dabbing it with a pot of sugar glue.

"Right," thought Riley. "One of you stole the pie recipe. It's time I tried to find out who."

Blake Cupcake

Lemony Melanie

"When the alarm sounded, I was in the Cheese Vault," Chef Jeff announced. "I didn't see a recipe for a pie."

"Hmm," thought Riley.

"Now if you will excuse me," said Chef Jeff, "I have pastry that must be dried."

"I was making my famous lemon curd tarts in my studio. The sprinklers turned my lemon sugar into a thick, sticky glue!" Lemony Melanie declared. "My poor fluffy puppy, Bowtie, is still stuck!"

"Oh no!" said Riley.

"I have sent for Bowtie to be rescued. Until then, don't go in there! It's not safe!"

Blake Cupcake blew on the glue. It had almost dried.

"I'm making a cake for Blueberry Sue," he said. "I haven't slept since last Thursday. What's a pie?"

He held the flower up and looked satisfied.

Riley needed to look at the clues. "Deputy," she called. There was no answer. "DEPUTY?" she shouted.

Riley looked around and saw Lemony Melanie petting Deputy. She was scratching her long nails deep into his fur.

"Come here, Deputy," Riley said, and whistled.

When Deputy returned, there were strange long blue streaks in his fur. They looked sticky. Could it be icing? Maybe glue?

Riley took out her notebook and looked at the clues. The blue lipstick from the pie recipe matched the streaks on Deputy's fur. Another clue!

Clues so far:

case of Blueberry Sue's missing pie recipe

Blue lipstick n a blue napkin

Yellow powder the fire alarm

"Wait here," said Riley, and she ran out into the hall.

Lemony Melanie followed her.

"I must tell you that I saw Blake Cupcake near Blueberry Sue's room!" she whispered.

Riley spied Lemony Melanie's long fingernails...

Back at Blueberry Sue's room, Dad had found a fluffy white dog. Its fur stuck up as if it had been blow-dried. Under its chin was a black patch, like a bow tie. It held something blue in its mouth.

"You must be Bowtie," said Riley. "And you've brought me a clue."

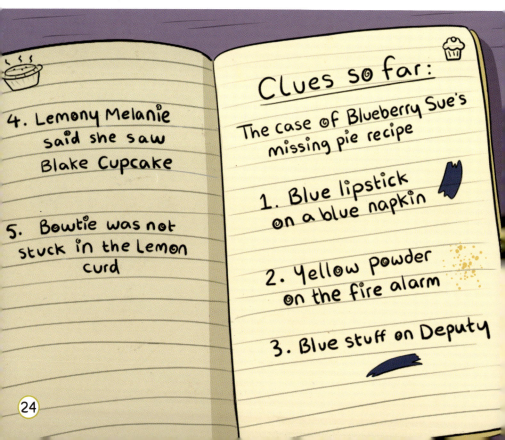

4. Lemony Melanie said she saw Blake Cupcake

5. Bowtie was not stuck in the Lemon curd

Clues so far:

The case of Blueberry Sue's missing pie recipe

1. Blue lipstick on a blue napkin

2. Yellow powder on the fire alarm

3. Blue stuff on Deputy

"I think I know who has committed this crime," said Riley.

Dad put on his police chief hat and was ready for action.

"Riley Rye to the rescue!" he cheered.

"Blueberry Sue," said Riley. "Your recipe was stolen by..."

"... Lemony Melanie!"

"Lies!" cried Melanie.

"The first clue was the yellow powder on the fire alarm. Someone blew lemon sugar into the alarm to set it off," said Riley.

"Only one person here uses lemon sugar!" said Chef Jeff. "I told you it wasn't me!"

"It wasn't you, Chef Jeff," said Riley. "But that wasn't the only clue."

"I found blue lipstick on Deputy's fur," Riley said.

"I don't even wear blue!" disputed Lemony Melanie.

"Look under your long nails,"

said Riley.

It was true! There was blue lipstick under her nails!

"It must have rubbed off when you took the recipe," said Riley.

"More lies!" screamed Melanie.

"And lastly, you told me that you saw Blake Cupcake near Blueberry Sue's room. But how could you have seen him if you were in your room, like you said?" Riley concluded.

"You and Bowtie weren't in your room at all!"

"Even more lies!" cried Melanie. "None of this is true!"

"It is true," said Police Chief Dad, stepping forward. "We found Bowtie in Blueberry Sue's room. She was bringing the recipe back!"

"It was you!" cried Blueberry Sue. "How could you be so cruel?"

"Alright. It is true," wailed Lemony Melanie. "I had to do it. No one watches my show anymore. I've tried everything! If you had made that amazing pie, no one would have watched me ever again! I saw a chance to get rid of you. I just wanted everyone to love lemons!"

"To Gingerbread Jail with you, you recipe thief!" said Police Chief Dad.

"Wait!" said Blueberry Sue. "Do you know what goes really, really well with blueberry pie?"

"No," said Lemony Melanie.

"Lemon curd," said Blueberry Sue. "Perhaps we could make the pie together?"

As the smell of lemon curd and blueberry pie filled the air, Riley Rye headed to the police car.

"It all worked out well in the end, didn't it," said Dad, taking off his police chief hat.

"Woof!" said Deputy.

"I agree, Deputy," said Riley. "I'm hungry too. Who wants some pie?"

Back at HQ, Riley and Deputy put all the clues into files. Deputy chewed on a piece of blueberry and lemon curd pie.

Riley put her notebook away, with the blue smear, the lemon sugar, and a photo of Bowtie chasing Deputy around the studio.

"Today was a good day for the truth, Deputy," she said.

Riley sat back and had a well-earned piece of pie. It had been a long day.

Riley Rye, Private Eye

1.   What was Blueberry Sue's TV show called?

2.   What did Blueberry Sue write her pie recipe on?

3.   Where was Chef Jeff when the fire alarm sounded?

4.   What did the sprinklers turn Lemony Melanie's lemon
     sugar into?
     (a)   A lemon paste
     (b)   A thick, sticky glue
     (c)   A slimy, yellow mess

5.   Why do you think Blueberry Sue let Lemony Melanie
     make the pie with her? Would you have forgiven Lemony
     Melanie?

©2020 **BookLife Publishing Ltd.**
King's Lynn, Norfolk PE30 4LS

ISBN 978–1–83927–012–3

Riley Rye, Private Eye
Written by Kirsty Holmes
Illustrated by Marianne Constable

An Introduction to BookLife Readers...

Our Readers have been specifically created in line with the London Institute of Education's approach to book banding and are phonetically decodable and ordered to support each phase of the Letters and Sounds document.

Each book has been created to provide the best possible reading and learning experience. Our aim is to share our love of books with children, providing both emerging readers and prolific page-turners with beautiful books that are guaranteed to provoke interest and learning, regardless of ability.

BOOK BAND GRADED using the Institute of Education's approach to levelling.

PHONETICALLY DECODABLE supporting each phase of Letters and Sounds.

EXERCISES AND QUESTIONS to offer reinforcement and to ascertain comprehension.

BEAUTIFULLY ILLUSTRATED to inspire and provoke engagement, providing a variety of styles for the reader to enjoy whilst reading through the series.

AUTHOR INSIGHT:
KIRSTY HOLMES

Kirsty Holmes, holder of a BA, PGCE, and an MA, was born in Norfolk, England. She has written over 60 books for BookLife Publishing, and her stories are full of imagination, creativity and fun.

This book focuses on developing independence, fluency and comprehension. It is a gold level 9 book band.